JUN 14 2012

DICKINSON AREA PUBLIC LIBRARY

J F Bracken, Beth.

Bracken, Beth.
Bloodfate

(Faerieground #3)

FAERIEGROUND

Bloodfate

Book Three

BY BETH BRACKEN AND KAY FRASER

ILLUSTRATED BY ODESSA SAWYER

STONE ARCH BOOKS
a capstone imprint

FAERIEGROUND IS PUBLISHED BY
STONE ARCH BOOKS
A CAPSTONE IMPRINT
1710 ROE CREST DRIVE
NORTH MANKATO, MINNESOTA 56003
WWW.CAPSTONEPUB.COM

COPYRIGHT © 2012 BY STONE ARCH BOOKS

ALL RIGHTS RESERVED. NO PART OF THIS PUBLICATION MAY BE REPRODUCED IN WHOLE OR IN PART, OR STORED IN A RETRIEVAL SYSTEM, OR TRANSMITTED IN ANY FORM OR BY ANY MEANS, ELECTRONIC, MECHANICAL, PHOTOCOPYING, RECORDING, OR OTHERWISE, WITHOUT WRITTEN PERMISSION OF THE PUBLISHER.

LIBRARY OF CONGRESS CATALOGING-IN-PUBLICATION DATA IS AVAILABLE ON THE LIBRARY OF CONGRESS WEBSITE.

LIBRARY BINDING: 978-1-4342-3305-9

SUMMARY: SOLI ENTERS FAERIEGROUND TO FIND HER FRIEND.

BOOK DESIGN BY K. FRASER
ALL PHOTOS © SHUTTERSTOCK WITH THESE EXCEPTIONS: AUTHOR PORTRAIT © K FRASER AND ILLUSTRATOR PORTRAIT © ODESSA SAWYER

PRINTED IN THE UNITED STATES OF AMERICA IN BRAINERD, MINNESOTA.
102011
006406BANGS12

"Wishes come true, not free."

– Stephen Sondheim, Into the Woods

For Valarie, who wished me away, and wished me home. -b

For the Fraser sisters: you are all a mother could wish for. -k

Long ago, a kingdom was
founded in Willow Forest . . .

The kingdom welcomed Calandra as their queen. The king deserved love and happiness. He was a good faerie, maybe one of the best. The wedding was beautiful. It was a time of goodwill and joy. The kingdom rejoiced.

Then tragedy happened. The faerie kingdom fell quickly into ruin. Only one thing could fix it.

Hope.

Chapter 1

Soli

The faerieground is beautiful and scary.

As soon as I'm here, I wish I wasn't.

My wish isn't the kind of wish that sent Lucy away. That wish was spoken and not true. Or not really true, anyway.

This wish is different. A true wish. A secret inside wish.

I try to cover it up with bravery. I try to turn my skeleton to steel, so nothing can hurt me. I try to be fire, so nothing can stop me. I try to stand bravely in the forest.

My mother always said I was brave, but I never believed her. After all, I spend so much time hiding, in the shadows. Not being brave. I don't think of myself like that.

My mother is brave, and my brother even more so. It might run in the family, but I'm adopted. My birth mother could have been brave. I don't know. I never knew her.

My mother says when I was a little girl, I would walk right up to the road, wait for cars to pass, and walk across. Just like that.

Also, when I was a little girl, I would introduce myself to strangers. I would smile and put out my hand and say, "I'm Soli. Who are you?" So maybe there's something brave inside me after all.

Maybe it was the small, brave part of me that wished Lucy away and then also the small, brave part of me that followed her here.

And I know that it is the small, brave part of me that takes the first small step into the faerieground.

When I feel something watching me, and I start to run, is that the brave part of me or the scared part?

Does it matter, if it's all to find Lucy and bring her home?

Chapter 2

Lucy

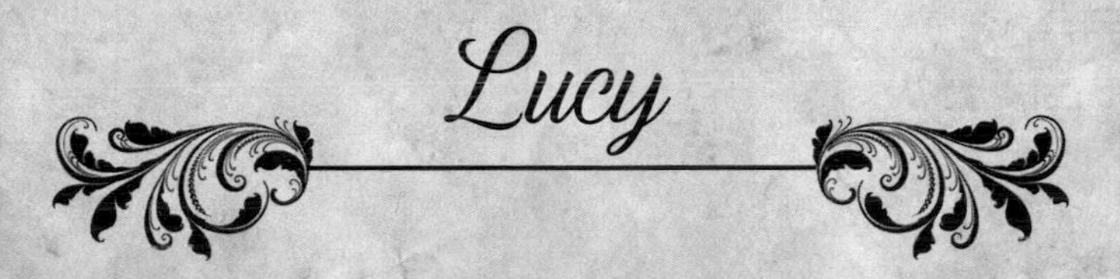

I can't believe I ever complained that my room at home was too small.

Now that I'm spending my second night in a prison cell, that little room at home seems like heaven. This cell smells like mold. It's dark and I'm freezing. I'm miserable. And I'm afraid. How long will my life be like this?

Kheelan is sleeping on his side of the cell. He's been here a while. He's used to it. But I can't sleep here.

I hear voices through our tiny little window. Footsteps, walking faster and faster. When the voices get closer, I can hear what they're saying.

"Yes, the dark one," a man's voice says. "She's here."

"Here? But how—" a woman begins.

The thumping of my heart drowns them out as they move farther away.

The dark one. That's what they keep calling Soli.

The dark one is here, the man said.

Soli, here? Has she come to find me?

"Kheelan, are you awake?" I whisper.

I hear his body moving on the floor. "No," he says.

"I need your help," I say. "Soli is here. We have to find her. I don't know if she can protect herself."

"Soledad is here?" he asks. I hear him shift in the darkness. "Are you sure?"

"I heard the guards talking," I tell him. "Can you get me out of here?"

He laughs. "If I could get you out, wouldn't I get myself out first?" he says. But his voice has changed. I can tell he's thinking about it.

"Then get yourself out," I say. "And find my friend. She needs our help. She can't do this on her own. Once you find her, you can come back for me."

I don't trust Kheelan. Not completely. After all, he's in prison, and all I know is that he angered the queen.

And he doesn't trust me. Not completely.

But we're all we have.

"Fine," he says. "I have to come up with a plan."

Chapter 3

Soli

What is it, what's chasing me?

How much longer can I run?

And where is Lucy?

Chapter 4

Lucy

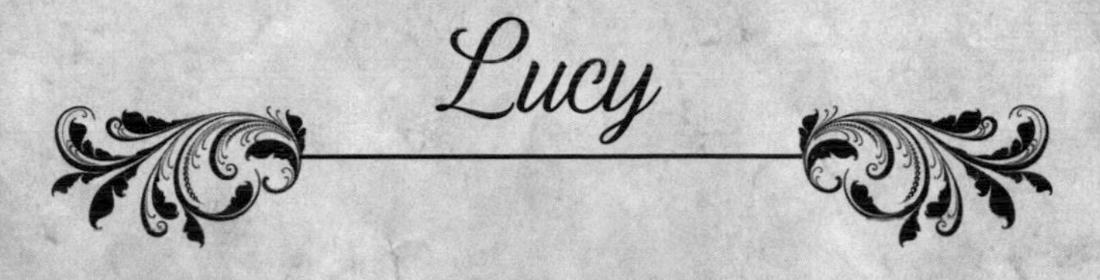

It seems like hours pass in the cold, cobwebby silence of our cell.

Then, suddenly, Kheelan screams. "Guards!" he yells. "The girl, the human! She's escaping!"

"What are you doing?" I whisper.

"Play along," he says. He yells again, "Guards! Hurry!"

Heavy footsteps pound up to our cell's door. Iron keys slip into the locks. I hold my breath. The door opens, and Kheelan launches himself at the guards, pushes past them, is gone.

Chapter 5

Soli

The thing that is chasing me through the forest, its footsteps pounding behind me, chases me straight to a cast-iron gate.

Then it is gone. The forest is quiet.

It has led me here. Maybe it was chasing me. Maybe it was herding me to this place.

My clothes and shoes are soaked and muddy from my run. I wipe sweat from my face and look around.

Beyond the gate is a bright green garden. The wildflowers are familiar but not quite right, like flowers in a dream.

And beyond the garden is a river, and beyond the river is the castle.

And Lucy must be inside that castle.

So that is where I need to go.

Chapter 6

Lucy

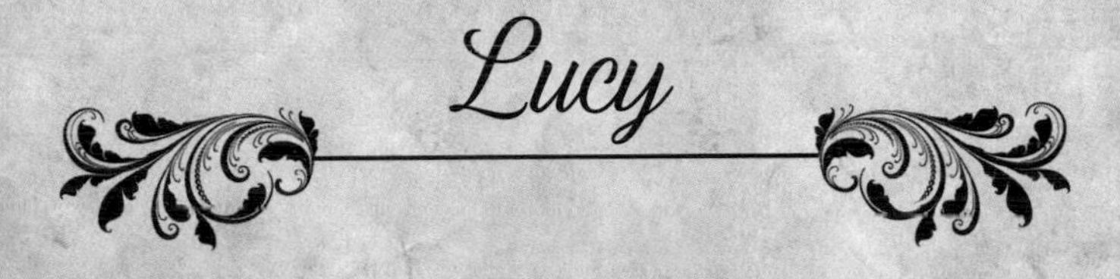

After Kheelan escapes, the guards take me to Queen Calandra.

They aren't gentle at all. They're mad at me. They think I helped him. They think it's my fault. I don't deny it. I don't say anything.

Last time, they took me to talk to the queen in the throne room. This time they take me somewhere else. They drag me deeper and deeper within the palace. It's not a palace like I always imagined, beautiful and golden. It's more like a dungeon, all of it, or a nightmare. The floors are dirty. Spiders—and worse—nest on the walls. The few lit candles are bent or broken.

It seems like it used to be beautiful.

It seems like something bad must have happened here.

The guards push me inside a room and slam the doors.

This must be where she lives. There's a fireplace, and a squat velvet sofa next to a lantern, some bookshelves. It's comfortable-looking, homelike. Fresh-cut flowers sit in a pretty vase upon the mantle.

There's a painting of the queen over the fireplace. She's holding something. A baby?

A tall figure stands in the soft light.

It's Queen Calandra, of course, and I can already tell she is angry.

The queen's eyes look even blacker in the shadows against her fair skin. Her thin wings hover over her shoulders. Her crown, made out of twigs, makes her look painful, and also in pain.

The guards have left me alone with her. I am afraid, but I know I need to be brave. So I decide to play dumb. Gain her trust.

"Where is Kheelan?" she asks me.

"That crazy guy who escaped?" I say. I shrug. "I have no idea. Last time I checked, crazy people don't, like, tell you where they're going when they escape from prison."

"My guards say you didn't try to run," she says. "Did he tell you he was leaving? Why didn't you go?"

"He told me he made you mad," I say, meeting her eyes. That's true, at least. "That's the last thing I want to do. Why would I try to escape with him?"

Queen Calandra sits down on the sofa. My eyes drift to its soft cushions. After more than a day in a stone cell, all I want is a comfortable place to sit. As if she can read my mind, the queen says, "Come. Sit."

I hesitate only for a moment before doing what she says.

This is the closest I've been to her. She leans close to me, brushes hair out of my face, smiles sweetly. Then she whispers, "There is punishment in my kingdom for liars."

I feel my blood turn cold.

She goes on, "If I find out that lies came from your pretty mouth, you will suffer times three. Understand?"

I swallow hard and nod. "Yes," I say. "I understand."

She gets up and paces silently. I look up at the painting above the fireplace. It's the queen sitting on this same velvet sofa. She is holding a baby. A dark-haired, dark-eyed little girl. The baby is wearing a necklace. I recognize it—it's just like my mother's pendant.

And the baby's eyes remind me so much of Soli.

Chapter 7

Soli

No matter how far I walk, the castle doesn't seem to get any closer.

It just gets more frightening. It's dark, dirty, crumbling. Not what I ever would have imagined a faerie castle to be.

The necklace around my throat feels warm, like it could burn me. Still, I tuck it into my shirt. Its warmth bounces against me as I run.

Just as I'm ready to give up, I hear footsteps behind me. I close my eyes and stand still. I don't have the energy to try to outrun anyone now. I hold on to Andria's necklace.

Then I hear my name.

I drop my necklace. It dangles near my heart.

When I turn, a boy is standing there. He smiles. "Don't run," he says.

He has beautiful, sharp features and dark, dark hair. It shines under the moonlight. When he takes another step closer, I see his green eyes. And after another step, I see his wings.

"Your friend sent me," he says. "Lucy." He smiles. "I can see you're still afraid," he says. "But you don't need to be. I'm here to help you."

“Who are you?” I ask, my voice hoarse.

He smiles again. “Kheelan,” he says. “My name is Kheelan. And I’m on your side.”

At first I think for some reason he means the fight between me and Lucy over Jaleel from school. The fight that made me make the wish that sent her here.

“There are many of us on your side,” Kheelan goes on.

“Who—who are you fighting against?” I ask.

He frowns. "There's so much you need to learn," he tells me. "We don't have time right now. You need to get to the queen."

"Yes," a voice says. I gasp and turn. Guards surround us in a matter of seconds. Kheelan looks like a wild animal, not ready to be caged in. This isn't part of his plan.

"We are the ones they fight against," one of them says, stepping forward.

"And we're here to bring you to the queen," says another. "She's been waiting for you."

Chapter 8

Lucy

*She sends me back to my cell,
empty now without Kheelan there.*

I sink down, put my head on my knees, and cry. Then, thank goodness, I fall asleep. I don't know how much time has passed when I wake up, but light is streaming through the cell's small window.

Just after I wake up, two guards come in to get me. This time they are gentler.

"Where are you bringing me?" I ask as we walk down the hall. I don't want to go back to her room. I'd rather be in the throne room than in her private space. For some reason, she's more frightening there.

"The throne room," one of the guards says. Her companion shoots him a look, but the first guard just shrugs.

When they throw the doors open to the throne room, the first thing I see is the queen. She looks angrier than ever. "The next ten minutes will test you, light one," she tells me. Her voice is almost a growl. She gestures to the guards and says, "Put the girl into the silence box."

The guards grab my arms and drag me to a glass box.

"You'll be able to see, but unseen," the queen says. Then she slams the door closed.

Through the box, I watch as more guards walk in. One is holding Kheelan down, struggling. Soli walks right behind him. Her chin is up. Still, she looks scared.

I pound on the glass. "Soli!" I scream, loud—my voice makes my ears ring. "Soli!"

She can't hear me. She doesn't look at me. The queen laughs. I'm a spectator to my friend's fate. This is my test.

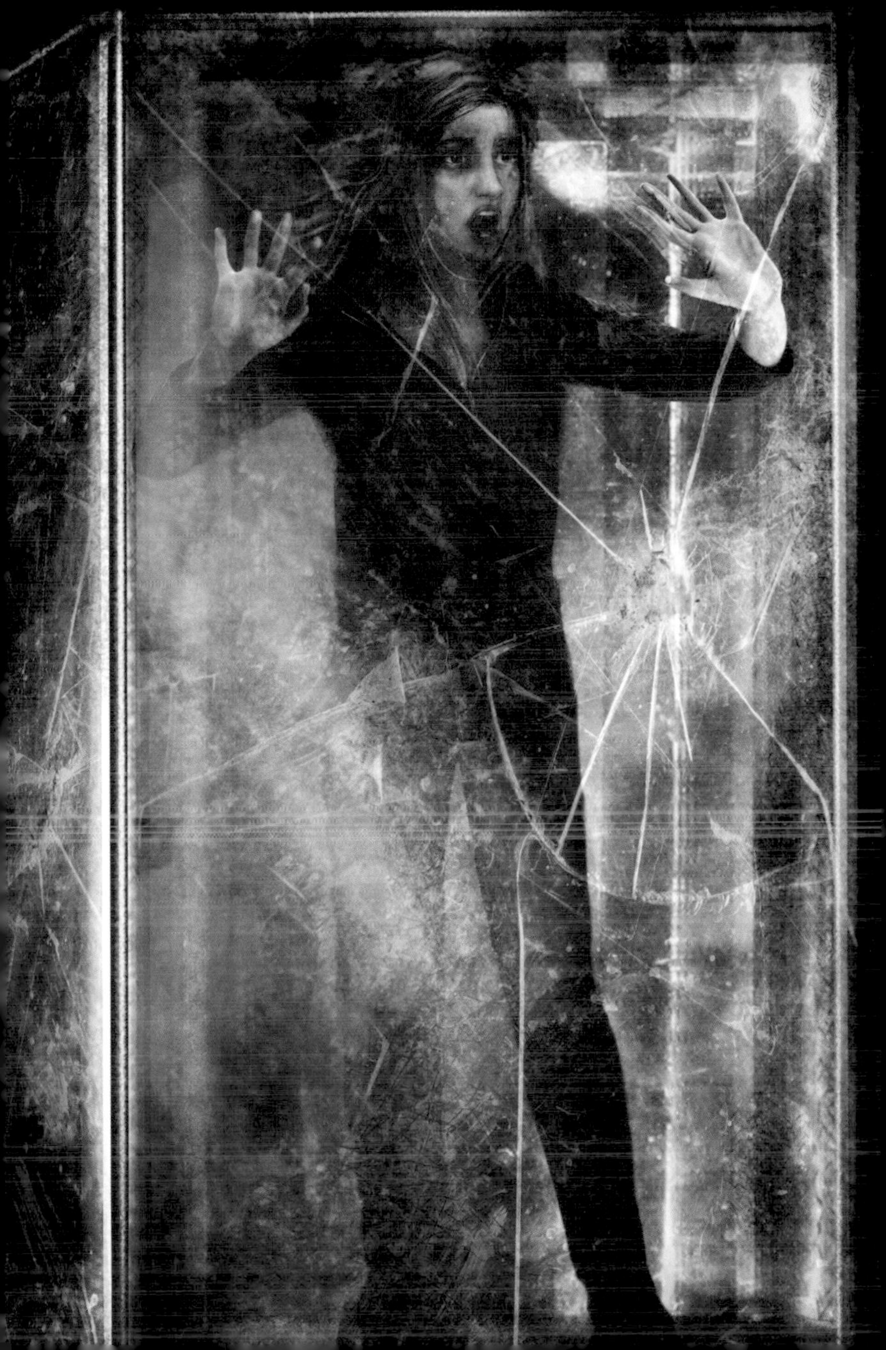

“Welcome,” the queen says to Soli. “Kheelan, welcome back.”

The guards force Kheelan to his knees in front of the Queen. Soli’s eyes go wide, watching his struggle.

My best friend looks tired, like she hasn’t slept in days. Her clothes are covered in mud. Her backpack is slung over her shoulder, just like after a school day.

“I know why you’re here,” the queen says.

"To get my friend back," Soli says. Her voice shakes, but it's clear.

The queen laughs. "Undo a wish made on faerieground?" she says, shaking her head. "That won't happen."

Soli's hands go to her throat. "I didn't mean to," she whispers. "It was a mistake. I was angry."

The queen laughs again, a bitter, angry chuckle. "A mistake?" she says. "I know mistakes." She glares at the guards and Kheelan. "Leave us," she says.

“No!” Kheelan yells, struggling to his feet. But the guards pull him out and slam the door. I can hear his cries coming from the hall.

And without him in the room, I am suddenly more afraid than ever.

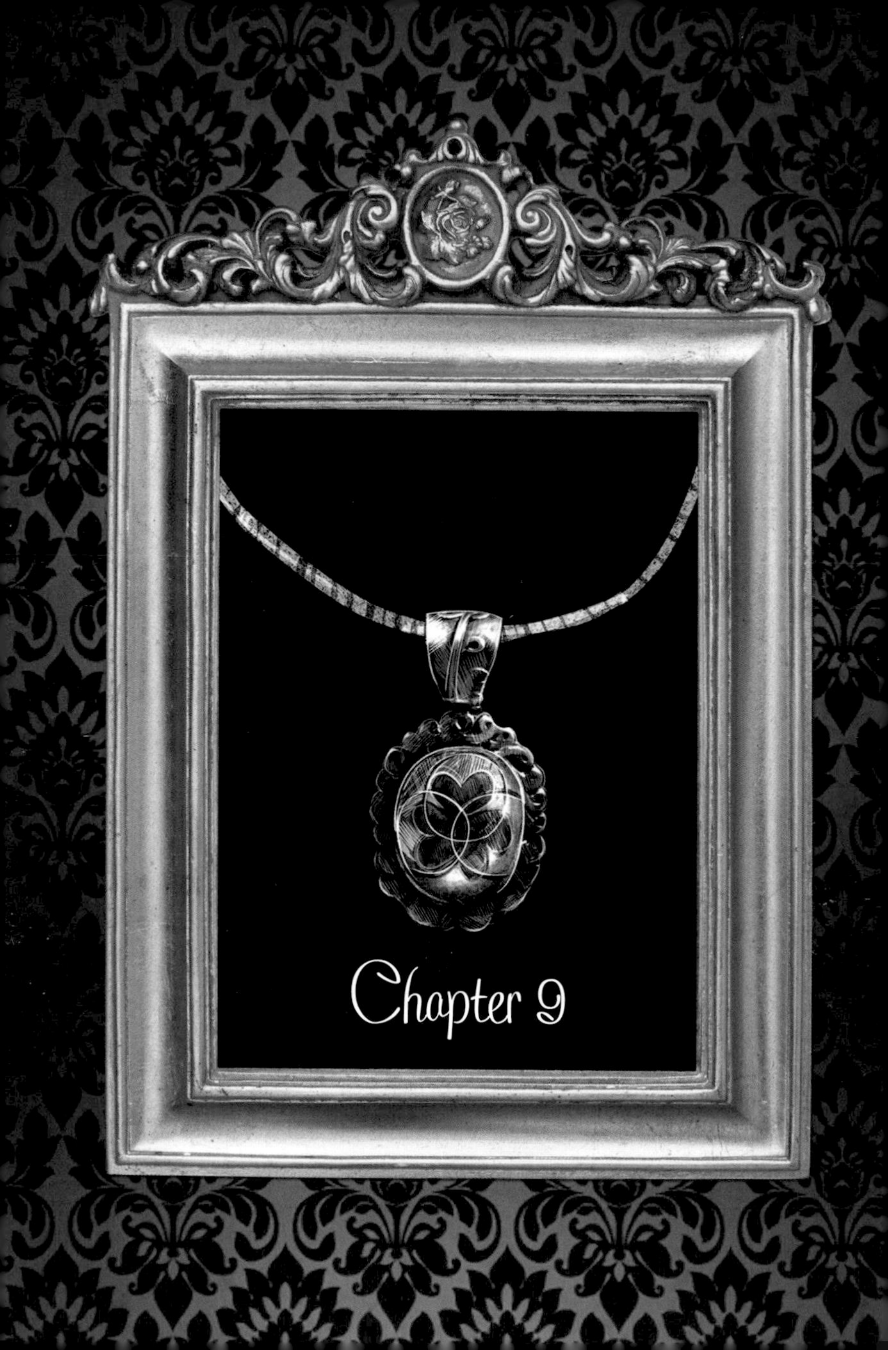

Chapter 9

Soli

We are alone now, the queen and I.

She returns her gaze to me. "So you want your friend back," the queen says. "What would you do to get her back?"

I try to steady my voice, to make myself seem more sure. "I'd—I'd do anything, I guess," I say. "Like I said, it was a terrible mistake. I'm sure you'd understand."

The queen glances at a tall glass box in the corner. "Would you promise to never see your friend again?" she asks.

I frown, thinking.

Never speak to Lucy again? Never see her? Never laugh with her?

Then I stand up straight. "If it meant she was safe, yes. I'd do anything."

She raises one dark eyebrow. "Then I have just the job," she says. "I'm going to send you to get something for me. Something that belongs to me. Something that was taken from me." She opens her mouth like she has more to say, but she stops.

"What is it?" I ask.

"The Dark Crown," she says. "It's hidden underneath the Black Lake. Only a human can retrieve it, but it is mine."

She's lying, but I don't know what she's lying about. I assume it's about who owns the crown, but I don't care. If getting it will make Lucy safe, I'll do it.

"If I get it, can I see Lucy again?" I ask. "Can we go home?"

"You have my word," the queen says.

"I need a guide," I say. "I don't know this place at all. Someone has to help me."

"Two birds, one stone," the queen murmurs. Then, louder, she says, "I'll send the boy with you. Kheelan. And if he escapes, you'll suffer his punishment instead. You have two sundowns."

"I want to see Lucy before I leave," I whisper.

The queen laughs. "Get out," she says.

Chapter 10

Lucy

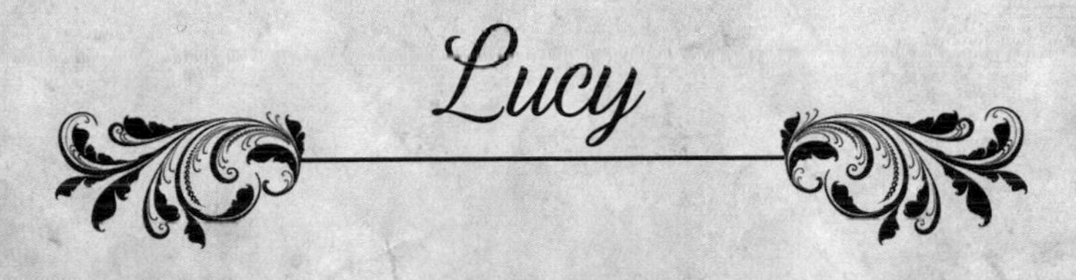

Soon I am back in my cell. I don't know where the queen sent Soli, but I'm starting to think both of us will die here.

Chapter 11

Soli

Kheelan and I walk for miles.

He knows his turf. He climbs rocks and trees like nothing I've ever seen before. I struggle to keep up with him. I keep worrying that he's going to run off into the woods and leave me alone. After all, what reason could he have to help me? But he doesn't leave me behind. He helps me every step of the way.

The forest is my forest, only it's not. I know it but I don't know it. I keep thinking I recognize things—a stream, a pile of rocks, a particular tree—but then when I look closer, it's not the same at all. Still, I can tell I'm in Willow Forest. But I know I'm nowhere near home.

The sky is lightening with sunrise when he stops and grabs my hand. "Right over there, do you see the smoke?" he asks, pointing.

Red smoke curls on the horizon. "Yes," I say. I brush sweaty hair out of my face. "What is it?"

"That's where the Ladybirds live," Kheelan tells me. As we get closer, the smoke fills the sky. "Do you know them?"

"No," I say. "Who are they?"

He pauses, then says, "They're our wise ones."

"Like the elders or something?" I ask.

He laughs. "You could say that," he says. "Some of them are five centuries old."

I gasp. "Are they—are they faeries, like you?"

But before he can answer, a loud voice says, "This is Ladybird land. Who are you?" A woman wearing red steps out from behind a tree. She's aiming a bow and arrow at us.

"I am Kheelan, of Roseland," Kheelan says. "And this is Soledad—"

“I know who she is,” the woman says. And she bends down, as if she’s bowing. When she straightens up again, she doesn’t meet my eyes.

“We are going to the Black Lake,” I say, trying to be brave. “The queen asked me to—”

“The queen?” the Ladybird says. “She can’t have the Dark Crown, if that’s what she wants.”

Nervous, I reach for the necklace around my throat. When I pull out the pendant and rub it between my fingers, Kheelan takes a step back. “Where—where did you get that?” he asks.

I look down and drop it back beneath my sweater. "Home," I say. "It's Lucy's mom's. She sent it with me when I came to find Lucy. I don't really get why, but—"

The Ladybird smiles and interrupts me. "I'm sure she knew what she was doing," she says. Then she gestures toward the smoke. "Come. Follow me."

She stalks off through the woods, and we follow behind her. Kheelan says, "That was—"

"Surprising?" I say, cutting him off.

“To say the least,” he says. “Soli, the Ladybirds are seer faeries. That’s part of why they stay secluded.”

“Creepy,” I say, watching the woman ahead of us. “I wouldn’t want that. To know so much, about everyone.”

“Nobody does,” he says.

The Ladybird leads us to a camp made up of tents built from twigs and leaves. The red smoke is coming from the center tent.

There are no men faeries here, so right away, I feel Kheelan's discomfort. But they don't notice him. They all stare at me.

"Motherbird will see you now," the woman who led me here says. She nods at the tent. "Your friend must stay outside."

The tent is full of smoke, but I see a figure inside. "Come in," a rich, deep voice says. An old, wrinkly hand reaches out from the smoke. "You are here for the Dark Crown," she says. It isn't a question.

"Sort of," I say. "I'm here to save my friend."

"The Dark Crown will save your friend?" Motherbird asks. "Tell me how."

I take a deep breath and tell her the whole story. Even the embarrassing part, the part where the boy I like kissed my best friend and I, angry and jealous and hurt, wished her away. Then how I traveled here, how the fireflies showed me the way. Then the chase through the woods, and Kheelan in the palace grounds. The queen, with her frightening eyes and the human-sized glass box.

Even the necklace, which now burns against my skin. I pull it out and show it to her.

"Can you help me?" I ask.

The woman cocks her head and looks at me. "I can bring you to the Black Lake, and I can help you get the Dark Crown," she says. "But you must never let it touch that woman's hands."

"The queen?" I ask. "But she said it was hers."

"It isn't," Motherbird says. "It is yours."

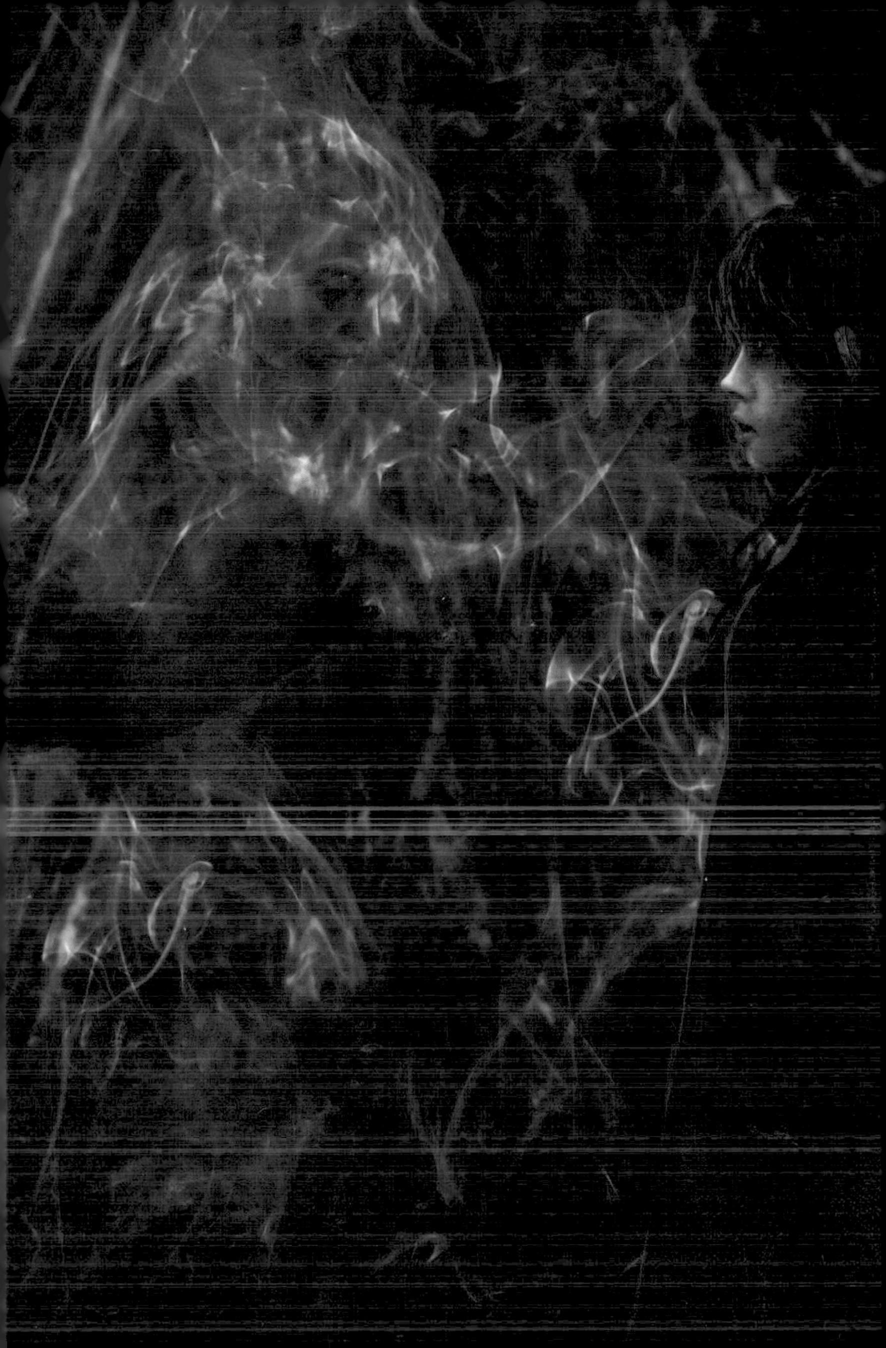

Chapter 12

Lucy

They bring me to her rooms again.

She is angry. I can feel her anger before they even open the door. I hear a bottle break against the stone floor. One of the guards knocks, but she screams, "Wait!"

Someone is in there with her. Someone with a low voice. I can't hear what the low-voiced someone says. I can only hear the queen. "The Ladybirds found her first," she is saying. "That's what you're telling me. That the Ladybirds found her. Again."

The voice says something in a soft, reassuring tone.

But the queen just laughs, a wild, crazy, angry laugh.

"That's ridiculous," she says. "Of course they know who she is. Even if she doesn't have the necklace, any idiot can see she's my daughter. And the Ladybirds know everything. Those old witches know. They know because they're the ones who took her from me."

The guard knocks again. "Should we bring her back to the dungeon?" he asks through the door.

The queen throws the door open. "No," she says. "Bring her in." And when she stares at me this time, all I can see are Soli's eyes.

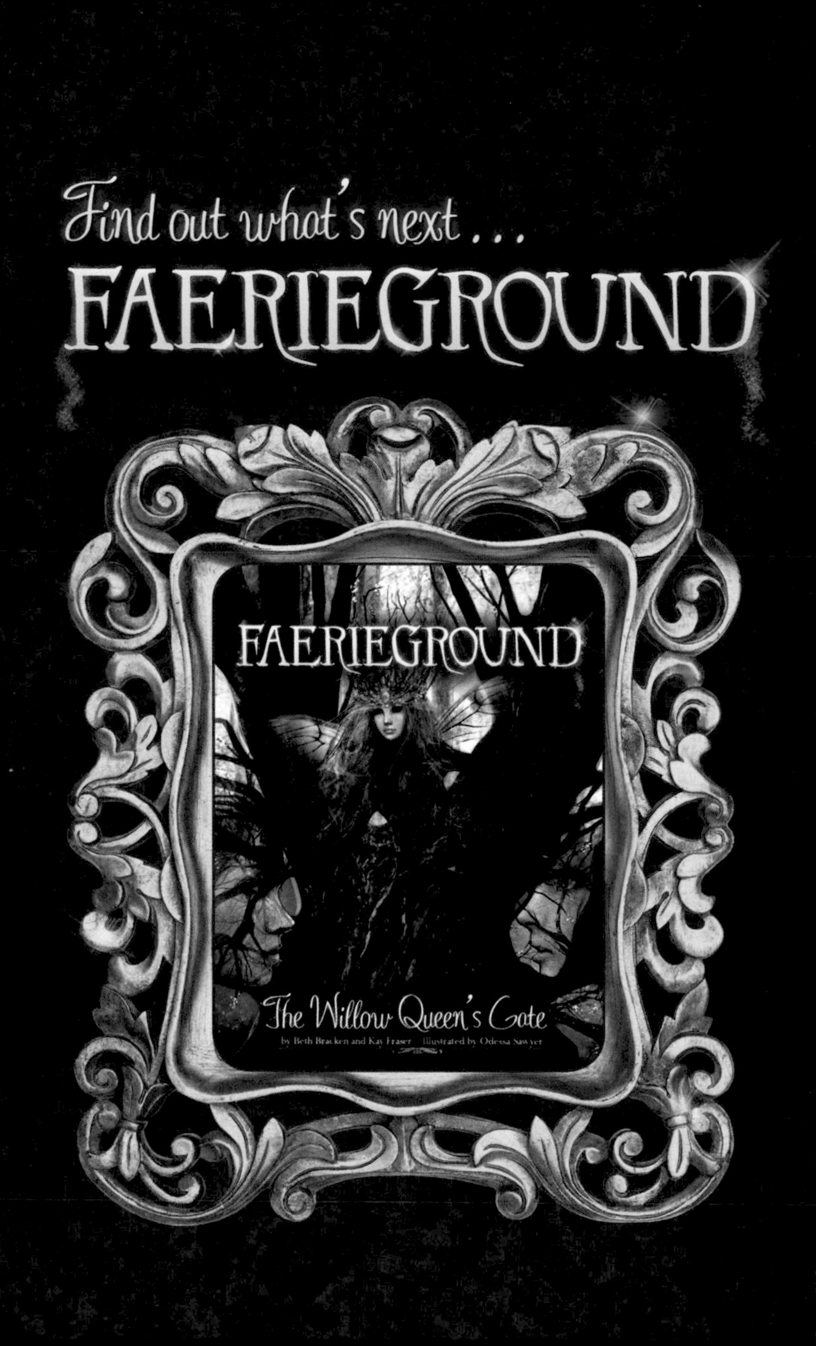
Find out what's next . . .
FAERIEGROUND
FAERIEGROUND
The Willow Queen's Gate
by Beth Bracken and Kay Fraser illustrated by Odessa Sawyer

Don't give up hope.

Soli and Lucy think they know their own stories. Their stories are each other's. But once they enter faerieground, everything changes.

As Soli travels to recover the Dark Crown and save her best friend, she learns more about her own story. And with the help of a mysterious stranger, Lucy finds out about a story that will change one of their lives forever.

Fate. Lies. Truths. And love. How will Soli and Lucy finish this story? And will the faerieground kingdom survive the telling?

Beth & Kay

Kay Fraser and *Beth Bracken* are a designer-editor team in Minnesota.

Kay is from Buenos Aires. She left home at eighteen and moved to North Dakota—basically the exact opposite of Argentina. These days, she designs books, writes, makes tea for her husband, and drives her daughters to their dance lessons.

Beth and her husband live in a tiny, crowded bungalow with their son, Sam, and their Jack Russell terrier, Harry. She spends her time editing, reading, daydreaming, and rearranging her furniture.

Kay and Beth both love dark chocolate, Buffy, and tea.

Odessa

Odessa Sawyer is an illustrator from Santa Fe, New Mexico. She works mainly in digital mixed media, utilizing digital painting, photography, and traditional pen and ink.

Odessa's work has graced the book covers of many top publishing houses, and she has also done work for various film and television projects, posters, and album covers.

Highly influenced by fantasy, fairy tales, fashion, and classic horror, Odessa's work celebrates a whimsical, dreamy and vibrant quality.